Gideon Elliot

The Good Bitch

Surprising Erotic Discovery

BDSM Erotica

WARNING

This book contains sexually explicit scenes and adult language. It may be considered offensive to some readers. This book is for sale to adults ONLY.

Please store your files wisely where they cannot be accessed by underage readers.

About the Publisher

4Fun Publishing, a member of **BLVNP Incorporated**, 340 S. Lemon #6200, Walnut CA 91789, info@blvnp.com / legal@blvnp.com
NOTE: Due to the highly emotional reaction of some people to works of erotic fiction, any email sent to the above address that contains foul language or religious references is automatically deleted by our anti-spam software and will not be seen. All other communications are welcome.

DISCLAIMER

Please don't be stupid and kill yourself. This book is a work of FICTION. Do not try any new sexual practice that you find in this book. It is fiction and not to be confused with reality. Neither the author nor the publisher or its associates assume any responsibility for any loss, injury, death or legal consequences resulting from acting on the contents in this book. Every character in this book is over 18 years of age. The author's opinions are not to be construed as the opinions of the publisher. The material in this book is for entertainment purposes ONLY. Enjoy.

The Good Bitch

Surprising Erotic Discovery
BDSM Erotica

By: Gideon Elliot

© **Gideon Elliot 2015**
ISBN: 978-1-62761-438-2

Chapter 1

Rachel banged her knee and scraped her elbow as she reached under the dumpster outside the Korean grocery store, but she managed to get her palm around the baby kitten she'd seen run under it and that was hiding there all by itself. Gently now she retracted her bare arm, keeping the hand holding the kitten suspended midway between the pavement and the bottom of the dumpster -- in order not to hurt the baby -- but the physics of that move insured more scrapes to her arm, a knock on the elbow, and a kink in her shoulder.

It was that time of evening between day and night when, although it is not darkest, yet it is most difficult to see things - the violet hour, the violent hour.

It was foolish, perhaps, to have stopped when she was late already, but she had long ago lost the reputation for being sensible, and it often got her into trouble, but she was ruled by her impulses. That's what Larry said. And that's why she needed him always to be looking after her and cleaning up her messes. But it never worked, and she always did something stupid again. She never learned. She didn't know what she would do without him.

* * *

He was surprisingly undisturbed when she got home. She knew that if she wasn't there when he got back from the garage, he didn't like it.

"I'm an old-fashioned kinda guy," he explained one night after he'd smacked her around because dinner wasn't ready when he got home and the house was a mess. He'd had a long and hard day, and sometimes a guy loses his temper. He wouldn't be normal if he didn't.

"I mean, I work all day to support us, and all you gotta do, I mean all you gotta do is keep up your end of the bargain, right? I mean that's what you wanted, wasn't it? Just when I come home, my slippers are out and there's a hot meal ready, and the house is a place I can be proud to say I live in it. And if you fix yourself up a little, try to look a little pretty, hey, that's icing on the cake. You know what I'm sayin'?"

"I do Larry; you're right. I'm sorry."

"I know you are," he said, taking her in his arms. "What am I gonna do with you?"

"I'll get better, Larry. I mean it. I want to."

She was looking up at him, now, wishing he would kiss her, and he did. A frisson of electricity passed through her and her body fell limp against his.

"That's it baby. Papa's home," he said and he slid his hand down her back beneath her cutaway jeans and started circling and teasing her budding aureole and then plunged in. She gasped. Her eyes glazed over.

* * *

He threw her onto the bed spread eagle, face down, and pinned her there with the might of his arms and knees.

"Tell me what you want me to do."

"I want you to fuck me."

"Tell me where."

"In my pussy."

"Where?"

"Up my pussy."

He circled her wrists with his fists and pulled her arms back. She felt as if her shoulder blades were cracking.

"Where?"

"Up my pussy," she repeated beginning to whimper.

He pulled her arms more. She began to sob.

"Where do you want me to fuck you, bitch?"

"In my pussy," she cried.

"Where?"

The pain was becoming excruciating.

"Up my ass."

"Again."

"Up my ass."

"Because I'm a pig."

"Ask for it, pig."

"Please fuck me up the ass."

"Beg."

The pain was intense.

"Please, Larry."

"Please what?"

"Please fuck me?"

"Where?"

"Please fuck my ass. Oh, please fuck my ass. Fuck my ass."

His cock was like a dagger poking at her now, and his breathing was wet with spittle on her neck as he tore into her flesh with his teeth.

"Tell me why."

"Because I'm a shitty, worthless little bitch and need to get fucked up the ass."

He ploughed into her. She screamed until the pain crashed like lightning, and then everything caught and turned upside down as in an inverting mirror and the pain turned to an ecstasy of pleasure she had forgotten, and she screamed as he stabbed her repeatedly, fucking her ass and digging his fingers into her arm pits and grabbing her breasts in fistfuls and scratching her nipples with his calloused finger tips until he collapsed on top of her and she almost couldn't breathe.

"You're gonna feel that all day tomorrow," he crowed, "and you're gonna know for sure whose bitch you are."

"I'm your bitch, Larry," she said, mindless with adoration.

"Damn straight you are," he said lifting his body off hers and swatting her ass. She rolled over.

"Get the hell outa that bed, bitch, and into the bathtub."

She obeyed instantly. He followed her, and when she was stretched out in the empty tub, he took hold of his still waning tumescent cock, and standing above her pissed a long, hard, golden stream of piss all over her. She quivered.

"You like that, don't you?"

"Yes, Larry."

"Now wash, for chrissake. You smell like a goddam street bitch, a fucking fire plug where every dog can go to piss," he said, getting into his jockeys. "And don't wake me when you get in bed. Or better still, maybe you better sleep on the floor tonight."

Chapter 2

In the moments before she fell asleep, Rachel promised herself things would be different. She was going to do a better job at everything.

She got up early the next morning, losing her balance when she tried to get out of bed only to find she was already on the floor. She prepared the coffee, poured him a glass of juice, cut the English muffins with a fork and had them ready by the toaster, poured out some Chocolate Puffs into a bowl and some milk into a pitcher - he didn't like it when the container was on the table -- and started a new jar of Marshmallow Fluff.

She set a dish of milk under the sink. She looked around the kitchen. The kitten was huddled in between a cabinet and the side of the refrigerator.

"C'mon," she whispered, squatting in front of it.

But it wouldn't move and she managed to take hold of it and carry it over to the dish of milk.

She had time so she lingered in the bathroom after her shower. She examined herself in the mirror. While never considering herself beautiful, she found that although she was barely twenty-four, she'd really lost whatever allure she used to have. She had put on weight, her hair was shapeless and without buoyancy, and she had become careless about her body hair as well and her skin was all bristly. Her panties, large white cotton things, had holes in them so her pubic hair stuck out in patches. Her bra had the dinginess of poorly washed underwear. She took a new tank top from the drawer, lime green, and pulled on a pair of cutaway jeans. She noticed her upper arms; that they lacked tonus, and to add to everything her sneakers were cheesy, and her thighs were beginning to be, too. It was not a good start. The promises she made to herself last night seemed impossible to keep, and she would have sunk into a deep depression, but she caught herself just in time. That would be no way to greet Larry. He didn't need to begin the day burdened by her grimness.

She was lucky; he woke in a relatively good mood and did not pay too much attention to her except to remind her that he was going to the automotive exhibit at the convention center after work, and wasn't sure when he'd be home, and that he might bring Mark home for dinner with him, so he wanted her to be a good little homemaker and have something good ready and not shame him in front of a buddy.

"Thanks for reminding me, Larry."

"You should keep a list or something. I shouldn't have to. Oh, one more thing. I got something for you just in case you forget."

She looked at him.

"Forget what, Larry?"

"Strip."

"Larry?"

"You deaf? Do what I tell you to."

She did.

"Turn around."

Without warning he stuck a butt plug up her ass. Several straps radiated out from it. He turned her around and belted one set around her waist, and brought the other set up over her cunt so that it was inaccessible, and buckled that set to the belt. Then he locked the buckles with a little key on his key chain.

"Get your clothes back on."

She did and looked at him questioningly, but afraid to speak.

"Just to help you remember how things are around here. Think of it this way: you're a bitch whose cunt is off limits and outa service."

And before she could say anything, he said, "Come on and give me a goodbye kiss," but it was not his lips or his cheek he offered but his hand. She bent and kissed it.

He scruffed her hair.

"Be a good bitch, baby," he said, and tweaked her by the nipple.

* * *

He must have known she played with her clit and pussy sometimes since he never did her there, and sometimes she was dying for it. But now, it was no longer an option. She'd have to get used to it and focus all her attention...somewhere else. That was probably what Larry had in mind when he locked her out.

He'd been right when he'd said she'd think about it all day, how he fucked her ass last night. She kept remembering it, feeling it again, each time dissolving into impossible desire. That and the plug up her butt now made her burn. Every time she moved she could feel him stretching her out more. She called him at the garage just to tell him how much she wanted him, but he told her to lay off, he was at work

She wanted to do something special. She wanted to show him how submissive she could be, how much she wanted to please him. So after shopping for dinner - she'd fry pork chops tonight with hash browns and apple sauce and finish it off with chocolate ice cream - when she passed a beauty parlor, she got up the nerve to go in.

Hairdressers were faggots, everyone knew that. Larry always mentioned it. Some faggot swish of a hairdresser, he'd say, when they'd pass someone on the street who looked 'that way'. And he'd say it loud enough for the guy to hear, as if daring him to respond but confident that he wouldn't have the balls to.

Chapter 3

Linda looked up from the copy of *Elle* she was reading. To Rachel, she looked like she'd just stepped out of the magazine.

It was her job to be beautiful and, indeed, she was striking, and a certain hauteur about the eyes and confidence about the mouth added to the rhetoric of her beauty. Many of the women who got facials, manicures, pedicures, body waxing or just their hair done were in awe of her, even intimidated by her, and some, although only a very few of them actually admitted it, were in love with her.

It was generally good for business. Her customers wanted to please her; they took her esteem as a mark of their merit, and they did nothing to disturb her regard for them, which often translated into paying the prices the salon charged as if they were getting a bargain.

"What can I do for you?" she said as Rachel stood flustered on the other side of the mirrored counter.

"I'm not sure," she said meekly. "I don't know." She hesitated, held back by the fear of desire. "I want to do something about my hair."

The discomfort of others did not bring out tenderness in Linda, and she gave Rachel a hard cold look, but said nothing. And then Rachel had to wait as she turned her attention to a woman in spiked heels and a black pants suit, who gave Linda a credit card and a smile. The jacket was cut quite low in the front, and it looked like it was being worn over nothing but her voluptitude.

Without even looking at Rachel, who was trying to think of some way to get out of the store without totally humiliating herself, Linda pushed several buttons on the imitation Regency telephone sitting on the counter.

"Gabriel," she said in something like a throaty whisper, "perhaps you can come out front for a minute."

Then, looking not at Rachel, but through her, as Gabriel approached, she said, with a baby doll smile, but not exactly to her, "Perhaps Mr. Gabriel can help you."

He was a sight that would have brought out a lot of Larry's hostility – there was no doubt about that – and Rachel felt awkward, even disloyal just for talking to him. First of all, he was exceptionally handsome, hard-to-look-at handsome. And then, what he was wearing! You couldn't help looking at him, staring even. He wore a pale rose shirt with nearly invisible bright yellow pin stripes and a tie of plum color brocade. His sleeves flared at the wrists, and he wore several bracelets of silver and a gold watch with a plum-colored face that matched his tie, and a brown leather wristband. He had rings on nearly every finger, a particularly fascinating jade on his right index finger. His trousers were of a brown you could lose yourself in – she'd never seen such a color before – and they fit like a glove. His boots looked like they were made out of highly polished mahogany. They had a small heel and a pointed toe. His hair was thick, wavy, a dark sandy color. His smile, if anything could, almost put her at ease despite herself. He was wearing an earring, a ruby stud in a silver setting.

"Don't let Linda cow you with that Mr. Gabriel stuff. Everybody calls me Jerry. What can I do for you?"

"I don't know," Rachel stammered. "I want to look better. I thought, maybe, I might get my hair cut. It's kind of long and shapeless."

"If you come back in an hour. I think we can do something."

"An hour?" She was disappointed.

"I have someone on the chair now, Angel."

(Angel?)

"I want to do this and I'm scared to do it. If I don't do it now I'll never do it." The words came out despite her, to her mortification.

"Look," he said. "I'll take you as soon as possible, but that'll be around an hour. If you want to wait here, you're welcome to. The chairs are very comfortable. Linda will give you a magazine or you can just rest, relax and get into an easy frame of mind so you can be ready to let yourself experience something new."

Rachel sat; the chair was comfortable.

"Good," Gabriel said. "That's right, Angel, relax, let yourself drift. Nothing is fixed. There are so many possibilities. Just let yourself drift. I'll be back as soon as I can, and then we'll do something. Ciao, bella."

"Ok," she said, as if she had been a cranky baby who had finally been pacified. She began to breathe and everything became warm with a sleepy heaviness.

* * *

She felt his hand on her shoulder.

"Come on, dream girl. Cinderella time approaches. That's right. Come with me."

They went past a number of women (and one guy) covered in white smocks. Some were having their hair done, and some were reclining with a green clay mask over their faces. He took her into a private room and indicated she was to sit in a maroon plush barber chair. The room was bright but the light source was hidden. There were mirrors wherever you looked, even on the ceiling.

"Ok, Angel, what do you want?"

She blushed. "I was kind of hoping you could tell me what I should do."

"You want me to see you the way you'd like to see yourself, but you don't even know how that is, and then make you look that way, right?"

"Pretty stupid, huh," she said, and even laughed.

"No, not stupid at all. Don't talk that way. The way we know who we are or what we are or how we look is by how other people see us. What other people tell us about ourselves, that's what we tend to give out. So you want me to see you as you'd like to see yourself, and then make you see what I see."

"That's kind of crazy, isn't it?"

"I don't think so. Why call names?"

"Can you do that?"

He nodded

"But it's not only about your outward appearance, you know. It's not just about mirrors. It's about how you see as well as what you see. Have you ever been hypnotized?"

She got excited when he said that, but held it down.

"No," she stammered.

"How about this, then?" he said, "I'm gonna put you under, but just a little, just gently at first. See how it feels, and maybe later, we can go deeper."

"Ok," she said. "But what about my hair?"

"Nothing radical," he said. "Let's start by making it real short. See what your face looks like. Get used to it. Then as your hair grows in we can see what it wants to do. How's that sound?"

"Whatever you say," she said, and smiled.

"That's the ticket," he said. "Relax now. Marie's going to shampoo you. Feel her fingers working your scalp, getting all the way into you. It feels so good. Everything's going to be new. Let yourself drift. You know you can count on me. You're beginning to feel so light-headed. All that hair that just pulled you down is going to be gone. Your head's going to float. When you walk your whole body's going to float. You're feeling loose as a cloud. Free and floating."

She sighed with relief. Her eyes fluttered. Then they shut.

Chapter 4

Larry didn't like it at all, not at all, and when Mark left, he flew into a rage.

"What the hell got into you?" he screamed.

She stood silent, frightened and confused, dreading what was going to happen and resigned to it.

"Did I tell you to get your hair cut?"

She couldn't find her voice. He smacked her. "I'm talkin' to you. I want an answer."

"No, Larry," she whispered.

"No, what?"

"No, you didn't tell me to get my hair cut."

"Then how come you did?"

"I wanted to please you," she said, breaking into tears.

"Cut the crap. The only person you were looking to please was yourself. Make you feel like hot shit so all the fellas'll look at you."

"It was only for you, Larry."

He smacked her hard. "That's for lying to me."

"I'm not lying," she said, and the tears turned to sobs.

The next morning she had a bruise on her cheek and her shoulders were sore from sleeping on the floor.

Larry wasn't annoyed that she hadn't fixed him breakfast.

"I'll get coffee and something at the donut place," he said, quite gently. "You can use the bed when I'm gone," he said. "You gotta change the sheets today anyway."

"On second thought you know," he said, rubbing her feathery scalp, "maybe it don't look so bad."

She ought to have been grateful, and she said "Thanks Larry," but the way it came out surprised them both. It wasn't sarcastic, but it sounded like she didn't actually care what he thought, that he'd lost hold of her, and it disarmed him. She felt calm.

She slept for an hour after he left, but woke in a panic. She had made an appointment with Gabriel to get her arms and legs waxed and to talk about starting a new diet and an aerobics class. It was before...before...when she thought that Larry...but now it would only.... Even in her thoughts she couldn't finish a sentence.

But the trouble was Gabriel expected her. She'd made an appointment. She had to let him know she wasn't going to keep it. She could telephone to say she couldn't come, but what if he asked her why not, and then she'd get all tangled up telling a lie. Anyhow, it was beside the point because she didn't know the number, and she hadn't even noticed the name of the shop. She'd just gone in. Just like her, doing everything impulsively. If she'd just thought it over without rushing in, everything would have been a lot...better.

Chapter 5

Linda took one look and picked up the phone.

Gabriel wasn't surprised. He gave her his hand. She took it.

"Come with me."

Gabriel learned during their first session what the relationship between Larry and Rachel was like when under hypnosis the first thing that happened was that Rachel wet her pants and on questioning explained that Larry had locked her in a contrivance that made it impossible for her to urinate freely.

The second day, when she came back bruised, and when she admitted under hypnosis that she wanted to leave Larry, but was unable to because of her own insufficiency and because she was turned on – despite not wanting to be – by violation and that the force of pain brought her a raw sensation like nothing else she'd ever known, he understood the course of action he had to take with her.

He put her more deeply into a trance and told her she was like an onion. One layer of skin was wrapped around another, one layer of desire was wrapping around another, and each time you peeled off the skin, each time she surrendered to a desire, all there was underneath was another layer, all that remained was the desire again. There were only layers and layers of surface, and together they were going to peel off all the layers, one at a time, desire after desire, actualizing all of them until there was nothing left, neither surface nor depth, neither center nor periphery, neither desire nor the inhibition of desire. And then...

* * *

In classical Greek tragedy, actual violence occurred off stage. Only its consequences and effects were shown to the audience. No one saw Jocasta hang herself or Oedipus pull off her earrings and smash them into his eyes. A messenger told of the events, and then the blind and bloody Oedipus came out staggering mangled and enlightened, afterwards, awing the spectators with pity for him and fear for themselves at his shock of recognition and their own premonition of what unwanted revelation might be hidden from their sight that yet might be waiting to pull them up short.

So, here, too, perhaps we ought to let the violence of enlightenment and healing be the work of darkness, the practice wrought by a wise hand during sleep, so that waking comes to be what waking seldom is diurnally, but ought to be for most of us: the realization that a metamorphosis caused by the experience of dreaming has occurred which has translated us from the tangled mass of conflicting wishes we had been bound to admit constituted us into the graceful elegance and stark beauty we had always seen only in the hidden mirror of our secret awareness but never in the falsifying reflections of reality.

Let us draw a curtain here, too, then, to suggest there is a backstage for this drama, perhaps symbolic of the recesses of the mind. There, Rachel's necessary and hallucinatory sleep can go on undisturbed as our narrative turns away from her and travels elsewhere as the trauma of her transformation occurs.

* * *

o~Gabriel's Notebook~o

I knew something was wrong the first time I saw her, before I ever put her in a trance or probed her. How? I have a feel for things. Not good enough? Ok, how a woman as beautiful as she is could neglect... neglect? No, sabotage her beauty and subvert her personality has to have some kind of reason.

First time I laid eyes on her I thought to myself, *'This girl's in trouble.'*

There was a guy involved. There had to be, and the situation was potentially very dangerous. That was one of the reasons I started slow – just a simple haircut to begin with - one thing does lead to another – and that's why I included the post-hypnotic suggestion that she had to feel compelled to come back the next day for a facial and a waxing. I was afraid of what it might lead to. I knew there was a risk. Worse, getting beaten turned her on. It fed into something that I knew she could use much more constructively.

When I saw her the next day and she'd been roughed up, I knew I couldn't let her go back again. I put her under deeply, and took full control. It was a risk. I wasn't freeing her. I was just replacing his domination with my own for the time being. A risky homeopathy, I admit, but I felt I could work it.

Kirk wasn't happy when I brought her home. "We don't need a housemate," he said.

"I know that," I said, taking him in my arms, "but she needs a place," I said, punctuating my words with kisses, "where she can fall apart and put herself together."

"You mean where you can put her together."

"Don't be jealous."

"I'm not jealous, only I worry about your motives."

In response I took hold of his balls inside his well-worn jeans and pried his mouth open with my lips and filled the cavern of his mouth with my tongue until I felt him yield. And get hard.

"You can't have my domination all to yourself. Don't be so selfish."

"No sir," he said, his eyes glazing over as I squeezed his nipples.

"Or I'll punish you."

"Please, Sir."

"Until you remember there are boundaries which you may not cross."

"Yes, Sir."

"Now fuck me," I said, unbuttoning my shirt.

"Yes, Sir. Do you consider that punishment Sir?"

"Don't be a wise ass."

Chapter 6

The first night she didn't come home, Larry was torn between anger and anxiety. Actually he was afraid. He couldn't see calling the police to report her missing. He was a bastard. But he wasn't a fool. He didn't want the law poking around in his life.

"Maybe she's spending the night at a girlfriend's house," Mark suggested the next day after work when they went out for beer and subs when Larry found that Rachel still hadn't come back.

"She doesn't have any friends like that."

"How do you know?"

"She never goes anywhere. She doesn't get any telephone calls. I know her."

"During the day?"

"Hey now, what are you trying to do? My head's fucked up enough already."

"Relax. Have another beer."

They sat without talking, drinking.

"You know, you been kinda rough with her."

"What's that supposed to mean?"

"Well, how come you assume she's split? Maybe something happened to her."

"It woulda been on the news."

"Anyhow, maybe she needs some time alone."

"Where she gonna go?"

"How should I know!"

The night dissolved, and Larry didn't do anything except phone Mark, waking him.

"Probably best to let things take their course."

"What's that supposed to mean?"

"I don't know. Don't be too rough on her when she comes home."

"Yeah, but she's gotta know I don't put up with this kinda business. The bitch."

"Hey man, tomorrow's a work day. We both need some sleep."

Rachel hadn't come back by the time Larry left for work, and no one answered when he called the house during the day. Nor was she there when he came home that night.

This went on for several more days. He got so edgy that one night the cries of the kitten, which he wasn't feeding, got him so crazy that he threw it out the window. It landed on its feet, and with a "mirckirgernaur" directed up at him, scampered into the falling dark.

And then there was a note on the table as well as her keys one evening when he got home. Otherwise there was nothing changed. The few clothes she had were still there.

"I don't need them," she wrote. "You can throw them away or do what you want with them. Please don't try to find me. The chapter is closed."

The End

Here is a sample from another story you may enjoy:

GIDEON ELLIOT

TABOO EROTICA

HYPNOTIZED

3 IN 1 BOXED SET

I'D KNOWN Jason since we were kids. I've always admired him – so much that it sometimes overwhelmed me. My admiration began with the way he looked. I always just enjoyed seeing him. He was a scrawny kid at the pool in the summertime, but lithe. He was adorable. When I think of him now, as I remember him during the summer, many years ago, when we were both seven, I can still see him as we undressed in the bungalow our families shared in Rockaway. He looked, stretching himself out of his little wet speedo, like nothing so much as a plucked chicken.

In his early teens he was smart and snappy and thoughtful, dressed sharp, got into gym and working out, as well as folk music – he taught himself guitar -- film noir, the Marquis de Sade, differential calculus, Nietzsche, and automobile engines. Girls talked about him, giggling with desire. He was easy around them, affectionate, cuddly, and, although he dated, he never got tied down to one girl friend. But none of the girls he dated expected him to, and none of them lacked for dates with other guys.

What was really beautiful is that he allowed me to love him. He was glad to accept it; he didn't push me away. When I looked at him with wondering eyes, with helpless admiration, he just grabbed me by the shoulder and horsed around for a minute.

Then he'd smile in the friendliest way. I didn't feel the least bit ashamed for showing my devotion. I'm always at ease with him but there are moments when I feel the excitement shaking inside me like I do with no one else. He's noticed it. And he doesn't hold it against me.

He'd go nuts if he couldn't accept love, 'cause he's a guy that everybody's crazy about, and he even can stay friends with girls who are dying for him but he won't sleep with them.

***

WE WERE in Butler library. We were seventeen. It was after ten, and the place was relatively empty. I'd managed to read all of Mill's *On Liberty* and I was thinking about the various possible extents and limits of human responsibility. I didn't get anyplace solid in my thought. I was spacey, floating, feeling like I was thinking but unable, the next moment, to remember exactly what I had been thinking.

Suddenly I heard fingers snap in front of my face and I saw Jason grinning. He'd just finished an assignment in differential calculus. If I had just had to squeeze my brain into that mold for two hours, I would not have been smiling.

"Where are you, Buddy?"

"I'm thinking about the limits of social responsibility and how you determine how much control any person can put on another; or an abstract group, like society, on the individual."

"Did anyone ever tell you that you lose yer bloom when you think."

"Cut the shit," I said, laughing at how beautifully he could move me from one place to another without even noticing it. "Aren't you tired of calculus already?" I said. "You're thinking all the time, and you haven't lost your bloom."

"Let's get some coffee," he said, throwing his arm round my shoulders.

"And stay up all night?"

"Don't worry."

Well, when Jason says "don't worry," you don't worry.

I couldn't get enough of him. I suppressed my sexual desire in order to be able to keep being with him. He didn't mind how I felt, but still I didn't want to make him uncomfortable by putting him in the awkward position of feeling like demands were being made on him, or of seeming like he was rejecting me. Most of the time it worked. I forgot about how much I wanted him and just enjoyed being with him the way we were. I forgot my sexual desire, or maybe it lingered as a ground bass giving greater resonance to whatever we did. I had become like an anorexic. Something else was more important to me than eating.

If you enjoyed this sample then look for **Hypnotized**.

My Fair Master

Carnal Spellbound

Sweet Surrender

Hypnotized

Slaves of Sex

Decisions

***

I REALLY LOVE Reviews!

If you enjoyed this book, please share the love and don't forget to leave a review on Amazon or the site of any other retailer you purchased this book from!

I highly appreciate your reviews, and it only takes a minute to write & post one. I can't tell you how much this means to me!

You'll find the list of all my books on my Author Central page... just in case you'd like to leave a review for other books of mine you've read but didn't have time to leave a review.

*Amazon Author Central – http://www.amazon.com/Gideon-Elliot/e/B00DUYBEQC

One Last Thing, For Kindle Readers...

When you turn the page, Kindle will give you the opportunity to rate this book and share your thoughts on Facebook and Twitter. If you enjoyed my writings, would you please take a few seconds to let your friends know about it? Because... when they enjoy they will be grateful to you and so will I.

Thank You!

Gideon Elliot
gideon_elliot@awesomeauthors.org

About the Author

Gideon Elliot was born in 1981 in Wichita, Kansas.

He grew up in San Francisco and spends the greater part of the year, now, on one of the Cyclades Islands in Greece where he runs a jazz café, paints, writes poetry, and swims.

He has a small apartment in Greenwich Village, where he stays from the middle of November to the end of April and, during those months, manages an erotic men's clothing shop. He began writing erotic fiction at the age of fifteen.

You may also like the books by these authors:

Just Plain Bob

THE REDHEAD'S *Desires*

Hot Romance Erotica

Mary Jane stood in the middle of the sound stage dressed in someone's idea of what a woman would wear on an African safari. Khaki shirt and shorts with way too many pockets and a pith helmet. Thick socks and hiking boots completed the outfit.

Several men, similarly attired, were lying on the floor with fake blood smeared on them. A mousy little man who had been introduced to her as the director made a motion and the AD (assistant director) shouted, "Places everyone." There was some stirring and then everyone was still.

"All right people, this is picture," the director said, "Roll camera."

A second later the soundman said, "speed," and the director pointed at Mary Jane and said, "Action!"

Mary Jane took a deep breath and then looked around her and wailed, "Oh my God, they're dead, they're all dead. I have to get out of here."

She turned to the left and started to go only to be stopped by the sight of three African warriors looking menacingly at her. She reversed course only to find four more in her path. Several of the black warriors leaped at her, grabbed her and pushed her to the ground as she screamed. Hands clutched at her clothes, ready to rip them off of her and she twisted and turned and screamed as she tried to fight them off. Suddenly the director hollered out, "Cut!"

He turned to Kraven and said, "This isn't going to work. The woman is just too damned sexy."

"What's the problem?"

"Look at my Africans, there isn't a soft dick among them and on film it is going to stick out like a sore thumb."

Kraven nodded and then said, "I have an idea." Turning to Mary Jane he said, "You can see the problem, right?" She nodded an amused yes. "I hate to bring this up and normally I wouldn't, but I saw you in action yesterday and I know that you have a strong sexual appetite." He motioned around him, "All this is costing a bundle and the quickest way to get back on track is to get rid of those stiff cocks. You are a professional Mary Jane and you have some idea of what production times cost. What do you think, can you help us out?"

Mary Jane looked over at the African warriors; Joe was one and so was Max. "Okay, I'll do it."

"Good girl. Can I ask a favor?"

"What?"

"You know what out takes are, right?"

"Yes."

"As long as you are going to do it can I roll camera? I would like to film it for my own private library. I'd like to pick it up at the point where they wrestled you to the ground and have you act as if they are forcing you. After all, that was the purpose of the original scene. The only difference is that in the real movie Tarzan, played by Brad Pitt, he saves you before it happens. I'll even give an under the table, tax free bonus of say, twenty thousand?"

Mary Jane kicked and screamed and tried to fight them off, but they ignored her and ripped her clothes off her. "This would be Academy Award stuff if it was ever seen by the paying public," she thought as the last little wisp of clothing – her thong – was ripped off her. She opened her mouth to scream again and a thick, dark chocolate manhood was shoved in her mouth. Hands grabbed the back of her head and the dick started to slam her face. A mouth attached itself to her right tit and fingers started pulling on her left nipple. More fingers entered her and a thumb was pushed into her ass.

Her body tingled with that delicious "do me" feeling that she loved so much, but the professional in her said, "Fight it off, MJ, you are being forced here, play the part." She got one hand free and she beat on the chest of the warrior stuffing himself in her mouth and she kept struggling and trying to break free from them. He legs were pushed apart and she felt the first slab of meat pierce her outer lips and it felt so damned good.

She moaned around the dick in her mouth as the dick in her pussy began to pound into her hard and fast. In the back of her mind she felt it rear it's head, "Oh shit," she thought, "there goes my Academy Award" as her first orgasm washed over her. She felt the manhood in her mouth throb and she knew it was only seconds away from pushing a load down her throat. At that exact instant she felt the dick in her organ pulse and her insides were splashed by hot sperm.

"Oh my God!" her mind screamed at her, "They aren't wearing condoms!" and she really struggled and tried again to break free. Hands held her legs apart as another black warrior moved between them and pushed his hard lance deep into her. The pole in her mouth spit out it's offering and she was forced to swallow it all or choke. When the cock pulled out of her mouth she cried out, "No, please God no, you ca...." But another member was shoved into her mouth before she could finish saying "do me without rubbers."

For the next several hours Mary Jane Parker was stuffed with dick as one man after another humped her. She had stopped her struggles and her body welcomed the invaders. She had orgasm after orgasm as her legs wrapped around torsos and her fingers dug into butt cheeks. She screamed out in pleasure and begged the men to enter her harder and make her cum.

Mary Jane had so many orgasms that her body was drained of strength and she was exhausted. She was so tired that when she was positioned on her hands and knees and Max took her anal virginity her scream of pain didn't have any more steam behind it than one of her low moans of pleasure (Peter had been there, but with him only having three inches it could still be considered untouched). By the time Max had emptied himself in her ass, the pain had subsided and she was pushing her butt back at him. Max pulled out of her ass and the other six Africans lined up to pooper poke her.

When the last of the black warriors had finished packing Mary Jane's fudge, Kraven made a signal to the cameraman and the camera was turned off. And then Mary Jane really got worked over as the rest of the cast and crew took turns ramming their cocks into whichever hole they fancied. Cameraman, soundman, gaffers, best boy, key grip, dolly grip and the janitor who kept the sound stage clean all did her. By the time the dead safari members got up off the floor and unzipped, Spider-Man's slut wife had passed out from exhaustion.

If you enjoyed this sample then look for **The Redhead's Desires**.

Erotic Seductions

Jack Ryder

Tempted and Tamed

Corrupting the Choirboy 2

Willow's mom was in the front pew when I stepped forward to sing the solo anthem hymn just before the sermon. She has been sitting there every Sunday since her divorce five months ago. It seems like her skirt and dresses have been getting noticeably shorter over the past several weeks.

Today, Gabi Pribino is wearing a very short grey sweater dress. Although it appears fairly acceptable when she's standing up, it tends to ride way up her thighs when she is seated. As the intro to the anthem is being played, I noticed that I can see the crotch of her white nylon panties. I feel a wiggle between my legs because they are transparent and I can clearly see her bare gash.

As I begin to sing the first verse of the song, I'm feeling very thankful that I wore a very tight jock strap today underneath my clothes. Last week, I got a full boner when she spread her legs to flash her crotch at me. Even with my tight jeans on underneath the choir robe, I was pretty sure that the folks in the front of the church might have noticed the bulge in my robe. Today, I was taking no chances.

I tried my best to not stare at her as I started the second verse. Gabi was smiling broadly as she very slowly spread her legs wider apart. I could very clearly see the pink folds of her pussy lips because her panties were now sopping wet. I felt my dick twitch as I motioned to the organist to stop after the refrain rather than go on to the third verse of the song.

As the congregation arose for the prayer before the sermon, I made my exit through the side door as always and practically ran to the changing room beneath the back of the church. I could feel the sloppy mess of pre-cum in my jockstrap as I pulled my robe off over my head. I was just about to go into the restroom to relieve myself when I heard a chuckle behind me.

"I bet you go in there and jerk off...don't you?" The sound of Gabi's voice startled me. But the fact that it WAS Gabi's voice also sent a bolt of excitement through my rigid prick and I felt a small gush of warm fluid ooze into my pants.

"Oooh Geez," I gasped when I turned around to face her. Gabi was sitting on a wooden chair against the back wall. Her legs were spread apart and she no longer had her white panties on. "Do you like looking at my pussy, Jack?" she whispered. "Does it make you have naughty thoughts?" she purred. My dick was hard as rebar and throbbing painfully against my tight jockstrap.

"Yes...I mean...no...I don't have...nasty thoughts," I groaned. "So...You like looking at my nasty thing but you don't wish you could shove your dick in it?" She goaded me with a wicked snarl. "Yes, I do," I blurted out as my face turned fire engine red. "I mean...Oh God...what do you want?" I moaned pitifully. Gabi was staring intently at the bulge in my jeans. "I want you to take it out and show it to me," she told me softly as she pulled her dress up to her waist to fully expose herself to me.

"But...what if someone comes and sees us?" I gasped timidly. I hated myself at that instant for staring at her dripping wet gash. And for the visions racing through my head of sucking on that organ and then filling it with my rigidness. "We have half an hour until the service is over," she replied in a seductive tone as she dragged a finger all the way up her drenched slit. "Don't be a sissy," she goaded. "Let me see what a big boy you are."

"Ooooooh Gaaaawwwd," I groaned as I watched her bury two fingers into her flower to the hilt. I was trembling as I unbuttoned my 501 jeans. My hands were visibly shaking as I hooked my thumbs in my jockstrap and yanked it down as well. *"I'm going to hell for this,"* flashed across my mind as I stood there in the basement of the church fully exposed to this gorgeous woman in the chair. My dick was bouncing against my belly with each pounding heartbeat.

"Look at you, Jack...You do like my nasty organ," Gabi laughed in a nasty tone of voice. "Bring that over here and let me touch it," she purred. I was amazed that my feet started moving without any hesitation.

I had to reach down and hold my jeans up as I made my way to where Gabi was seated. "That is sexy, baby," she whispered as she reached out to wrap her right hand around my dick. She had a curious little smirk on her face as she saw that her small hand barely made it all the way around my girth.

"Ooooooh…" I groaned as she slowly pumped her hand up and down my prick. "I bet you think about my vagina when you jerk off," she hissed her taunt. "Yes…I do," I mumbled hoarsely. "SAY IT THEN," she yelled. "I think about you when I jerk off," I gasped without hesitation. "Good boy," Gabi chuckled. "And what do you want to do to me?" she whispered.

"I…ugh…ugh…want…ugh," Gabi squeezed forcefully on my dick before I could finish. "SAY IT," she yelled.

"I want to eat you and hump you till you can't walk," I screamed back. "Good boy," Gabi laughed wickedly. "Get on your knees and show me."

If you enjoyed this sample then look for Tempted and Tamed.

A Compilation of Love Stories

L♥ve
and
Lust
Erotic Romance

Amy Redek

With our meal over, she said, "This is my bed," pointing to the large palm leaves that I'd already noted, "and you'll have to sleep on the sand tonight. We'll get some more palm leaves tomorrow for you." So with that, she pulled the unburnt wood from the fire and went and settled herself down on the palm leaves, pointing to the sand next to her. So that's where I went and lay down, seeing her settle herself in the dim moonlight before we said our goodnights to each other.

She at least was wearing some sort of clothing whereas I was only wearing my shorts and I woke up sometime during the night feeling quite cold, and I must have rolled over to her to share some of her body heat, for I was cuddled up to her when I awoke in the morning. She must have known this but never said a word as I rolled away from her and got up and walked out onto the beach to see that my boat was still there. I even went and had a swim and on coming back to the shelter, saw that she had set out two small palm leaves that took the place of plates and on each, was a variety of fruit which appeared to be our breakfast.

With that finished, she wanted to show me over the island but I insisted that we salvaged as much as we could from the boat before it disappeared. And so that's how we spent my first full day on the island, by getting everything that I could off the boat. Lunch had just been nuts and fruit but for dinner, we toasted some spam to eat and she didn't really like the fact that I would only open up one can of tinned peaches. Taking it in turns to spoon out a segment to eat and then shared the juice to drink. She thought it was delicious and wished that I would open another but I stood by what I had said from the start that we would be parsimonious with the tinned food to make it last as long as possible.

What with spending the whole day ferrying this from the boat via the sail, we forgot about getting some large palm leaves for my bed and so, like the night before, I was to sleep on the sand again next to her. But like the night before, I was cuddled up to her like two spoons in a drawer, my body up tight to hers with an arm over her and I know damn well that she felt me when I woke up, for I had a massive morning erection and it was pressed up to her backside. I rolled away from her and went straight down to the sea and dived in to let the coolness of the sea to shrink my erection back down to its normal size.

Yet again, she never said a word but it showed when she said that before we tried to salvage more from the boat that we got some big palm leaves for my bed. I'm sure my face went red at her saying this but this is what we did after our breakfast. I am not going to keep repeating myself but breakfast consisted of the same fare every morning, so take it as read as to what we ate having already said what it consisted of.

So with my bed in place next to hers, we went swimming again to get the last of what could be transferred ashore. This was done by the end of the morning, and the afternoon was spent in building up a fire beacon that could be lit on seeing any vessel in sight. The extra advantage was the fact that I still had the Very Light and flares to send up if needed.

Now for dinner, we had plates to eat from and not palm leaves and the tinned chicken stew went down a treat as did the tinned fruit for dessert. The cheese, what I had left over, had now gone so mouldy as to be inedible and she was going to throw it into the sea but I stopped her as it would make good bait, for I had salvage my fishing gear which later came in full use for catching fish to cook and eat. I think I'm dragging this out a bit being somewhat reluctant to say what happened that night, but I suppose I'll have to.

We still had moonlight when we laid down on our palm leaves, me now having a T shirt to wear and not feeling the cold air so much. But it was her that rolled over to me this night and cuddled up to me and had her hand come over my waist. Now just with having her bring her body up to mine set my own body into a state of flux. With me feeling her breasts being up close to my back and her hand over my hip, aroused me, and my body gave out a shiver when her hand felt the front of my shorts. She felt what was there inside, a man's penis at a full erection and knew exactly what to do with it.

Her hand then moved and slowly undid each button on the front and with the front now being open, her hand went inside and…

If you enjoyed this sample then look for **Love and Lust**.

JOAN VEGAS

Hot Dates
Being Sandwiched
MFM AND RELATED ADVENTURES

HOT ROMANCE EROTICA

According to leading Sociologists, the number of American women who have opened their lives to intimate affairs has substantially increased in recent years. It is estimated that as many as 60% of all married women have had affairs. That's right... 60%!

Yes, that's still less than the estimated 70% of all married men who are believed to have had affairs, but it reflects the fact that growing numbers of women are reaching out for sexual variety in their lives.

Sadly, traditional secret affairs still usually bring with them feelings of guilt and anxiety. Yet, it is understandable that women, just like men, want their sensual lives to be fuller, they want "newness," and they want the excitement of experiencing different partners and different sexual adventures.

I have always been a proponent of variety in sexuality for both men and women. But, I have advocated that couples share in the development of new pleasures for each other, that they intentionally allow each other to experience extra partner and that they actively participate in providing extra partners "as gifts" for their primary partner.

Some call what I advocate "open marriage." While I feel open marriages are far better than the traditional "closed," monogamous marriage, I feel that husbands and wives can enhance the open marriage concept by periodically inviting others to join THEM in bedroom play. I encourage couples to explore the addition of another guy or gal to their love play as a way to take an active role in providing their spouse with extra partners while doubling that spouse's sensual pleasures.

For decades (centuries?) men have talked to their wives about bringing an extra guy to their shared bed. Many men fantasize about watching their wife being serviced by one or more other guys. Sometimes it is the woman who proposes such a threesome (MFM - male/female/male, or female-centered threesomes). But, more often than not, the wife is the "hesitant" party, turned-on by the idea, but "hesitant" to really give it a try.

The following are comments gleaned from letters I have received over the last few years from women who have opened their lives to extra partners... not within the context of affairs, but within the context of threesomes or open marriage agreements. I will let them tell for themselves WHY they enjoy this way of expanding their feminine potential.

Joan

If you enjoyed this sample then look for **Hot Dates: Being Sandwiched**.

DD WATSON

Punishing
PUPPET

HOT EROTIC HARDCORE

Her head floated from side to side as she willed her eyes open. Her eyelashes parted to allow light in, but there was only darkness. The drug injected into her held her still even though her legs and arms were free.

She began to remember how she came to be where she was. The ride in the car trunk was by far bouncy but warm. When the trunk was open, her Master was there but didn't assist her out of it only his driver and another male she didn't recognize hauled her out. Before she could assess where she was the driver placed a patch on her neck, and her world went black again.

Puppet was never one to dwell on any negative situation. She trusted her Master Troy, no matter how mad he was with her breaking his rules he loved her unconditionally.

Going to the island was a set punishment but Puppet saw it as a learning experience. One she plans on succeeding in to make her Master proud.

She took in a deep breath and slowly exhaled it. That seem to help because she was able to move her fingers and toes sending a tingling sensation through her arms and legs. Puppet felt a growing chuckle inside her as if she was being tickled under her skin.

A smile spread on her cheeks as she tried to remain still to avoid another attack.

"You're awake," said the voice of a male that sat on the floor right beside her.

"Yes," she moaned. "You can see me?"

"Well yeah."

"So—it's not dark in here?"

"No it's very well lit you're just wearing a blindfold and the drug given to you is slowly wearing off."

"Oh, so where is the light coming from?"

"Window with a view of the garden showing a lovely sunny day."

"Why aren't you wearing a blindfold?"

"Because I'm here to watch you."

"Oh, so I'm on the island?"

"That is correct."

"Where's my Master Troy?"

"I'm not at liberty to say Puppet."

"And you know me. Am I allowed to be asking you questions?"

"With permission."

"By you?"

"No, by my Master—Shawn," he said, glancing up at the green eyed male who handpicked him out of a dozen. Took ownership, making him his personal pet; he stood clean shaven wearing black jeans, biker boots and shirtless. His long black mane hung loose on his shoulders. Two men stood behind him both wearing leather pants black boots and chest harnesses with buzz cut hairstyles.

"Is Master Shawn training me because I disappointed my Master?"

"He is."

"Is he listening to us?"

"Yes."

"Is he here in the room with us?"

He was signaled to silence by Shawn hovering his fingers in front of his pet's mouth. Shawn sat beside Puppet and leaned into her ear.

"I'm right here Puppet." His accent vibrated through her ears as she took in the heavenly scent that radiated from his skin.

Puppet enjoyed the tender time she was allowed to spend with him even though she hasn't laid eyes on him yet.

"That will be all Peter you may return to your duties."

"Thank you Master." On hand and knee Peter crawled out of the room followed by one of the males. Turning his attention back to Puppet, Shawn took his fingers and traveled over her naked skin, igniting the sensation that tortured her a moment ago.

Puppet tried to keep a straight face but regaining some movement in his limbs she began to squirm and giggle. Shawn only watched as she didn't try to push him away but seem to enjoy the torment. He watched her nipples harden as he flicked them with two fingers. Then running them between her legs he felt the wetness building in the soft folds of her crouch. He brought his drenched fingers to her mouth and pressed them pass her lips where she sucked and licked them clean. He removed them and rose to his feet.

"Get her to her knees on the floor and face her to the bed," he ordered a male who moved quickly to perform his task. Jerking Puppet up, he forced her into position as Shawn instructed.

Shawn walked over to a duffle bag opened in the corner and removed a handheld whip. The handle was as long as his arm with nine tails all knotted. When he returned his attention to Puppet, still blindfolded on her knees, he didn't hesitate. When the first strike landed she let out a deep cry that ricocheted around them. He landed another that resulted in the same. He picked up the tempo and continued to strike her back and arse until the welts glowed a profound red.

"How many blows did I give you Puppet?" He asked watching her claw at the mattress. "Answer me," he snapped striking her again.

"Six—teen—Master."

"Splendid, most pets never count. Troy has been training you."

"Yes Master—my Master is good to his pet."

"A little too good, or you wouldn't be here Puppet."

"Yes Master."

He switched the whip in his opposite hand and walked over to Puppet, snatching the blindfold from her eyes.

"Turn around Puppet and place your arms on the bed for support but remain on your knees."

"Yes Master." She turned clumsily but managed, getting her first glimpse of the notorious Shawn. The man whom her Master said strikes fear in any pet who crosses his path. Why was she not afraid? Was he just playing with her? She caught his emerald eyes, which shot ice daggers at her. His chiseled looks could rival her Master Troy's.

"Troy mentioned you were hard-headed. Who said you could look at my eyes?"

Puppet caught on, but it was too late as he began to whip her chest, stomach and thighs. The pain was more intense, but she kept her arm on the bed and didn't try to run away. Her Master Troy whipped her in this same manner on different occasions, so she grew to accept her punishments no matter how unforgiving they were.

When he stopped, she collapsed onto the floor at his feet breathing intensely but not unconscious.

"Take her to the groomers and tell them I'll call when I'm ready for her."

The male lifted Puppet up as if she didn't weigh a thing and draped her on his shoulder carrying her out of the room.

Peter had lied to Puppet, who was hanging upside down. She glanced around the room and saw no window only a ceiling light, mirrors and two doors.

Once Puppet was gone the second door opened, and Troy walked in wearing his full business attire. Shawn turned and smiled at his old friend from school whose dreams mimicked his.

"So what's your conclusion?" asked Troy.

"She's knows what she wants. I never saw a first timer take what she took from me. Or—maybe I've become soft."

"No, it's not you, Puppet is without doubt atypical. I can do anything to her, anything I wish."

"Then why bring her to me? Apparently you have a handle on her."

"No, she's become hesitant and explorative, not asking permission."

"She's evolving?"

"It has been five years. And as I said she'd taken my treatments without complaint."

"Do you want me to train her to be a dominatrix?"

Troy fell silent as he glanced to the floor. He closed his eyes and remembered his devoted pet and how she found him. Shawn's strong hand rested on his friend's shoulder waking him from his thoughts.

"It's been a long trip for you both, come and relax with me and let the groomer spoil her. A good meal, drink and sucking will clear your mind to make a decision."

That brought a grin to Troy's face as he let Shawn lead him out of the room.

If you enjoyed this sample then look for **Punishing Puppet**.

WANT FREE COPIES OF MY BOOKS?

Just visit my blog and download free copies of my books:
http://gideon-elliot.awesomeauthors.org/gideon-elliot/